Lad   ers

Iz   ıts

To access the audio and digital versions
of this book:

1 Go to www.ladybirdeducation.co.uk
2 Click "Unlock book"
3 Enter the code below

ohRhYF9nN5

Notes to teachers, parents, and carers

The **Ladybird Readers** Beginner level helps young language learners to become familiar with key conversational phrases in English. The language introduced has clear real-life applications, giving children the tools to hold their first conversations in English.

This book focuses on verbs and provides practice of saying "I can. . .".

There are some activities to do in this book. They will help children practice these skills:

 Speaking    Listening*   Writing   Reading   Singing*

*To complete these activities, listen to the audio downloads available at **www.ladybirdeducation.co.uk**

Series Editor: Sorrel Pitts
Text adapted by Sorrel Pitts
Song lyrics by Fiona Davis

LADYBIRD BOOKS

UK | USA | Canada | Ireland | Australia
India | New Zealand | South Africa

Ladybird Books is part of the Penguin Random House group of companies
whose addresses can be found at global.penguinrandomhouse.com.
www.penguin.co.uk   www.puffin.co.uk   www.ladybird.co.uk

Penguin
Random House
UK

Text adapted from *My Little Pony* episode "Izzy Does It" by Hasbro Inc., 2023
This version first published by Ladybird Books, 2023
001

Licensed by:

Text and illustrations copyright © Hasbro Inc., 2023
MY LITTLE PONY and HASBRO and all related trademarks and logos are trademarks of Hasbro, Inc. © 2023 Hasbro.
The moral right of the original author/illustrator has been asserted

Printed in China

The authorized representative in the EEA is Penguin Random House Ireland, Morrison Chambers, 32 Nassau Street, Dublin, D02 YH68

A CIP catalogue record for this book is available from the British Library

ISBN: 978–0–241–61691–8

All correspondence to:
Ladybird Books
Penguin Random House Children's
One Embassy Gardens, 8 Viaduct Gardens, London SW11 7BW

Ladybird Readers

Izzy's Presents

Based on the *My Little Pony* episode
"Izzy Does It"

Picture words

Izzy

Sunny

present

bike

5

Izzy loves making presents.

Izzy makes a present for Sunny.

"Here is a present for you,"
Izzy says.

"I love it," says Sunny.

"Can you make us presents, Izzy?"
say the ponies.

"Sunny loves my present," says Izzy. "How can I make presents for my friends?"

"I do not know!" she says.

13

Izzy walks.

She sees a bike.

The bike is very old.

"Can the bike help me?"
says Izzy.

"Look!" Izzy says. "Now I can make presents for my friends!"

1 **Talk with a friend.** 🗨

What does Izzy love?

She loves making presents for her friends!

Can the bike help her?

Yes, it can!

2 Listen. Color in the words.

1
| Izzy | Sunny |

2
| makes | loves |

3
| old | bike |

4
| present | friend |

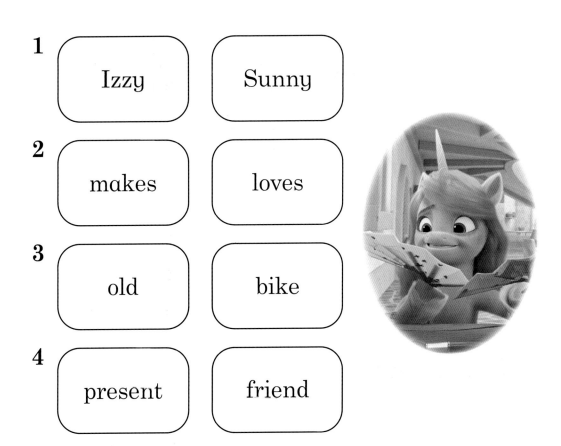

3 **Listen. Put a** ✓ **by the correct words.**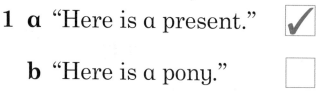

1 **a** "Here is a present." ✓

   b "Here is a pony." ☐

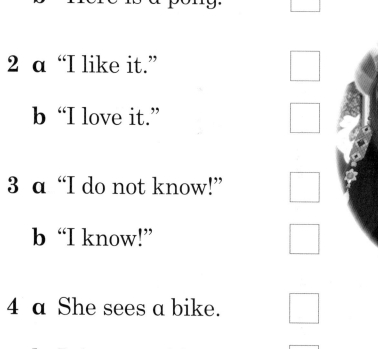

2 **a** "I like it." ☐

   b "I love it." ☐

3 **a** "I do not know!" ☐

   b "I know!" ☐

4 **a** She sees a bike. ☐

   b It is very old. ☐

4 Listen. Write the first letters.

1   present

2 bike

3   old

5 Sing the song.

I love presents.
I love making presents.
Here is a present for you!

How can I make presents?
Presents for my friends.
I do not know. I do not know.

I can see a bike.
A very old bike.
Yes, I know! Yes, I know!

I can make presents.
I love making presents.
Here is a present for you!